*Your train leaves, it's time to say goodbye*
*and now, oh! yes, now we truly die:*
*indeed, one can die from having been*
*so happy for so short a while.*

Verse taken from
*Encore une fois/Once Again* by Jacopo Serafini
*Atti segreti nel tempio del cuore/*
*Secret Acts in the Temple of the Heart*
Edizioni Croce, 2016

*The Friendship Surprise*
This edition published in 2022 by Red Comet Press, LLC, Brooklyn, NY

First published as *Uno due tre*
Original Italian text © 2021 Giorgio Volpe
Illustrations © 2021 Paolo Proietti
Published by arrangement with Kite edizioni S.r.l.
English translation © 2022 Red Comet Press, LLC
Adapted and translated by Angus Yuen-Killick

Library of Congress Control Number: 2021946569
ISBN (HB): 978-1-63655-028-2
ISBN (Ebook): 978-1-63655-029-9

22 23 24 25 21 26 TLF 10 9 8 7 6 5 4 3 2 1

Manufactured in China

RED
COMET
PRESS

**RedCometPress.com**

# The
# Friendship
# Surprise

Giorgio Volpe & Paolo Proietti

Red Comet Press • Brooklyn

For Little Red the fox, the most beautiful time of the year was the arrival of spring. The time was nearing when his friend Hazel, the dormouse, would wake from hibernation. Little Red was so bursting with excitement, he couldn't help but break into a run.

He only slowed down to have a think.

Every year, Little Red would celebrate
Hazel's awakening by preparing a surprise.

But this year was different. During the winter, Little Red had made friends with Brock the badger, and the two had become inseparable.

*What if Hazel's surprise this year is meeting a new friend?* thought Little Red.

Three friends playing together could be fun,
but Little Red wasn't sure about introducing Brock
to Hazel. *What if Hazel prefers him to me?*
Just thinking about it made Little Red feel sad.

So instead, he moved Hazel's teapot home to the
lakeside, in a field of daisies, feeling that
would be a much better surprise.

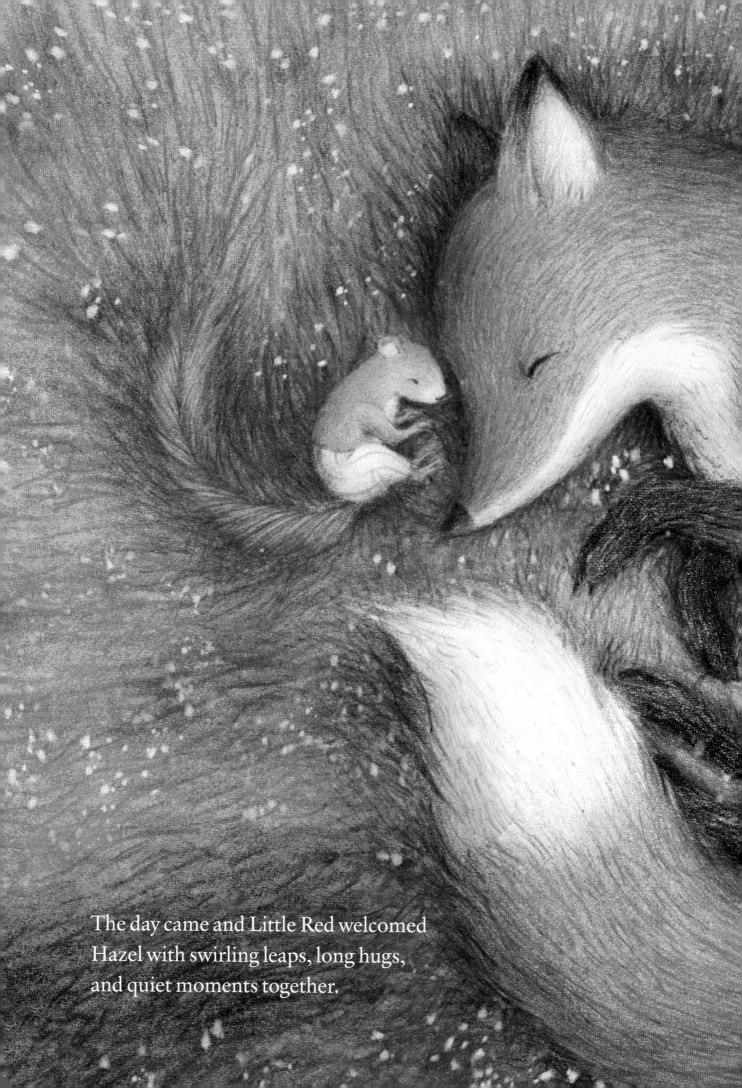

The day came and Little Red welcomed
Hazel with swirling leaps, long hugs,
and quiet moments together.

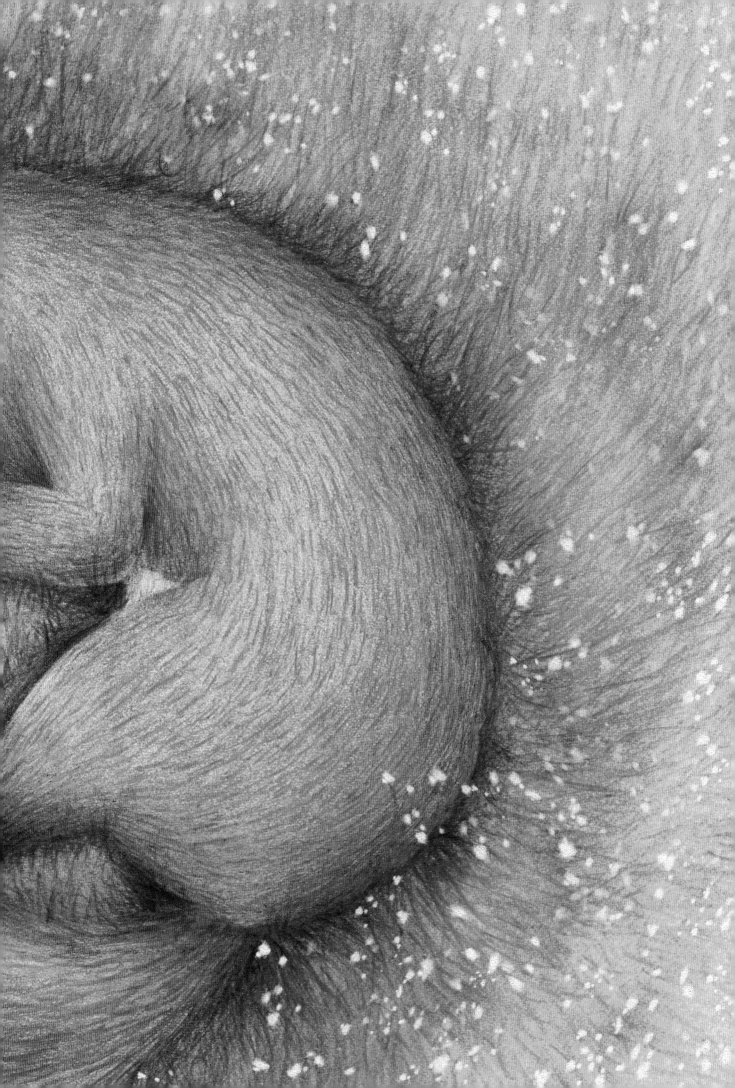

And that evening he took Hazel to admire the dancing fireflies.

"I missed you so much, Hazel."

" Little Red, the important thing
is we are together now."

The two friends resumed spending most of their days together, but in Hazel's eyes, Little Red was behaving strangely. Little Red never used to  be the first to leave, but now he always was.

One of their favorite games was picking strawberries.
It didn't matter who collected the most,
the important thing was to have fun.

But that day Little Red was distracted. He wished he
could talk to Hazel about Brock, but he just could not
find the courage.

Hazel watched Little Red wander off in thought and decided to follow.

When Hazel discovered Little Red was meeting with Brock, everything became clear.

The next morning, Hazel asked Little Red if there was something wrong, but Little Red avoided the conversation.

"What would you say if next winter I hibernated with you?"

"And your new friend, who will stay with him?" asked Hazel.

Little Red was speechless.

"Why haven't you introduced me to him yet?" continued Hazel.

Little Red curled up and responded nervously: "I was afraid you would not want to stay with me anymore and I would lose you."

Hazel hugged him. "That would never happen, Little Red. I'm sure we can *all three* have fun together."

At those words, Brock burst out of the bushes with a beaming smile.

"What are you doing here?" exclaimed Little Red in surprise.

"You were acting so strangely that I decided to follow you," replied Brock.

Hazel burst out laughing. The surprise was Little Red's, and a moment later Brock and Little Red joined in with Hazel's infectious laughter.

One, two, three,
and they all started playing together,
just as friends do.